For Maddie, Piper and Riley.
With special thanks to Team Cooper
- K.C.

For Motorbike Sue
- N.S.

Bloomsbury Publishing, London, Oxford, New York, New Delhi and Sydney

First published in Great Britain in 2018 by Bloomsbury Publishing Plc
50 Bedford Square, London WC1B 3DP

This 2018 edition produced for Scottish Book Trust

www.bloomsbury.com

BLOOMSBURY is a registered trademark of Bloomsbury Publishing Plc

Text © Katrina Charman 2018
Illustrations © Nick Sharratt 2018
The moral rights of the author and illustrator have been asserted

A CIP catalogue record of this book is available from the British Library

978 1 4088 6495 1 (HB)
978 1 4088 6496 8 (PB)
978 1 4088 6494 4 (eBook)

All papers used by Bloomsbury Publishing are natural, recyclable products made
from wood grown in well managed forests. The manufacturing processes
conform to the environmental regulations of the country of origin

Printed in China by Leo Paper Products, Heshan, Guangdong
13 5 7 9 10 8 6 4 2

Car, Car, Truck, Jeep

Katrina Charman   Nick Sharratt

BLOOMSBURY

LONDON OXFORD NEW YORK NEW DELHI SYDNEY

One for
the red bus,

one for
the train.

One for the pilot in her jumbo jet plane.

Honk, honk, beep, beep,

driving down the road.

Pass by the tractor
with its heavy load.

There goes a motorbike
weaving to and fro.

Stop at the
red light,

then *ZOOM*
off we go!

Chugga, chugga, choo, choo,
race along the track.

Pull along the carriages,
clack-clickety-clack.

Arriving at the harbour,
by the seaside.

Hop on the hovercraft,
such a **bumpy** ride!

Flicka, flacka, flicka, flacka, what's that in the sky?

Look! It's a helicopter,
buzzing on by.

Spot the yellow taxi
bouncing up
and down.

Climb slowly up a steep hill
on the way to town.

Rumble,
rumble,

scrape,
dig,

there's a dumper truck.

Digger lifts the bucket,
filled with dirt and muck.

Flashing lights
and sirens,
a police car
rushes past.

When there's an accident, they must get there fast!

Vroom, vroom, screech, roar, on the motorway.

It's time for bed now,
we've had a busy day.

Yaaawn sighs the red bus,
zzzzz snores the train.

"Sweet dreams,"
says the pilot in her
jumbo jet plane.